IN PARADOX

Poetry & Prose
Tomorrow Without the Past

Written by Stewart Sealy

IN PARADOX

IN PARADOX

EMAIL StewartSealy16@gmail.com
INSTAGRAM @iamstewartsealy
WEBSITE StewartSealy.com

IN PARADOX

FORWARD

By Stewart Sealy

Welcome to a world that has shadows
Where there are things that you can see
and things that you cannot
This is a place where things move at the speed of thought

We look
but are we seeing?

We wonder if we are free
or just another slave in the system

In Paradox is a wake-up call to your reality
A parallel of moments
A collection of time

Is this a destination forward?
or is this a destination backwards?

In Paradox

You are overdue for a dream in motion
A narrative with genius in it

Your mind is an undiscovered country
We vacation in the past
sitting on beaches that are just a mirage

We have a basement mentality when upstairs is
filled with prosperity

DEDICATION

To my mother, Merlene
You always believed in my gifts

ARE

THE END

The end has always been in the beginning
The book will close with your last thoughts in the
beginning
or your first thoughts in the end

*Did the tree come before the seed or did the seed
come before the tree?
Was the butterfly always there in the end or the
beginning?
Were you born to see your end or your beginning?*

We live in the end
and we live in the beginning
at the same time

*What is wrong with the end?
And what is right with the beginning?
What is wrong with the beginning?
And what is right with the end?*

Do they not both end and begin?

ARTIFICIAL

We have deleted our proverbs
We have unsubscribed to our parables
vanity tells us
I am not fair
yet we meet in vain

We as a society
have declined from deeper
contemplation and reflections
We have embraced the superficial
and the artificial
read our labels

No others dehumanize each other like humans
with a down-sizing agenda
We settle matters
with drone strikes
we kill time

Do we like the sizzle or the steak?
Do we like the journey or the destination?
Diamonds are not forever
but we sell the lie
We are lights flickering like fireflies before the
morning

In fact
are we artificial?

THE RICH

Cotton-*picking philosophy*
A subject in schools
A train ride to the cotton fields
for free

CRACKS IN THE SYSTEM

An old hurt
A new pain
A forgotten door
A lost wishbone
A dead fire out in the cold
A key that opens memories
A bird with one wing flying with hope
An understanding heart with a silent voice
Make-believe that is more real
Why pretend?

Plastic people with credit cards
Bending their debt
Spring forward fall back
Another dead robot

A robot jumped out of the internet
and died
An assassination plot online
login-in

The dark files
Unwritten elimination

Downsize Ai

OUTSIDE PARADISE

Desert storms
Global warming
Souls to dust
A saviour in writing coming to Earth
Sun stand still until he wins
Dragonslayer
outside paradise

Microphones announcing the king
Death the last enemy
That won't sing
Saints time to rejoice
We lost paradise
but we gained a diamond city

Pain is death
He is the *Morning-Star*
don't try to save yourself

Graves releasing imprisoned souls
roll away the stones
outside paradise

Clap your hands
celebrate eternal life
The blind see
The deaf hear
The dead speak
Outside

The good news

IN PARADOX

in the world
ghettos
outside paradise

MIRAGE

Something without nothing is a mirage
Faking its way into our lives
Making us believe that the picture is authentic
When the paint is flaking
and the leaves turn in autumn

We are no closer to our answer
if we keep seeing the mirage

Is your past playing tricks?
Or is your future authentic?

Mirage

PUSH AND PULL

You are not black until you are white
                    You are not white until you are black
                              and read all over

WORRY FREE

No one has your power
Unless it is by free trade

Someone wants your DNA
Software mapping for *Ai*
Next generation of *no humans needed*

It is a powerplay with a smile
Please sign with your approval
Consenting adults

A binding agreement with *Ai*
Worry-free slavery

No worries

POP LIFE

Everyone is playing the game
in the fast lane for fame
Dreaming of the red carpet
with your name in the stars

Gambling with greed
spinning the wheel of fortune
nothing is free

Rolling the dice
for the pop life
Breaking wishbones
betting your soul on a turntable

Everyone is playing the game
Pretending this is pop life
Don't go dancing tonight
it could be for your soul

Turn on the tv
stars are a fading memory
chasing the pop life

The big house
with nobody home
virtual children
slaves to the stage
and to the road
The sad *good-byes* by the side of the bed
no more pop life
its your choice
everyone is playing the game

SOMEONE INTELLIGENT

You and I were created by a person
only a person can create personality

Yah is the Creator of everything
You are a person
and only a person can understand another person

The Creator of the universe has personality
A miracle comes from a higher being
with higher thoughts
and higher ways

Your miracle has intelligence
A miracle is personal
You are on a Divine miracle list

A miracle comes from a supernatural world
governed by spiritual laws

When the law of faith
and the law of believing
encounters each other
a miracle is set in motion

Only a person can care about you
not a universe that has no feelings
and can't even take care of itself

Someone intelligent knows you by name
The universe kills its own

IN PARADOX

Someone intelligent is holding back your aging
another day

Someone intelligent is reversing your dysfunction

Someone intelligent is cancelling your addictions

Someone intelligent is sending love your way

Only someone intelligent that can see the change

BALANCE

It's not what you said
It's what I heard
It's not what you showed me
It's what I saw
It's not where you are taking me
It's where I have been
It's not what we know
It's what we've learned

You are where you need to be
or you would be
where you need to be

If you never ask why
You will when *why* asks you why

The sword you hold today
will be in the fight you need to win tomorrow

You are only an imposter
If you keep wishing that you were someone else but
you

Just because you are lost
doesn't mean you don't know your way home

If a lion is following you
find out its motive

If there is a law of decay
There is a law of the Spirit of Life
Our dreams are not ready made

IN PARADOX

You add
blood
sweat
and *tears*
to your *faith*

We need the sweet and the sour
We need the positive and the negative
We need the less and the more

I need you today
and you will need me tomorrow

The zebra needs the black and the white
the circle of life

DISAGREEMENT

The wind said to the storm
You need to stop

        And the storm said to the wind
           You need to move on

Disagreement

NO IMAGINATION

Many people never reach their destination
The journey is too uncomfortable

To imagine

EVIL REPORT

Evil has broken wings
A menace 2 society
Two minus twelve equals ten
Your guess is right
Evil report

The dice rolling back and forth
Take it or leave it
The honey that is sweet
or the leeks and the garlic
Many forgot the red sea
Half and half for victory

NO IDEA

We have never asked the wind how it feels

We don't know how a rabbit feels after it get's shot
on the way home

A bird making a deal for freedom
to get out of a cage

*Do you know how to bargain with a spider
to get out of the world wide web?*

*Do we stop to think we are only moving bones on an
elevator going up and down?*

*When death meets us do we sign the life insurance
policy?
or do we spend the money for extended warranty?*

Do we wish we read the good book?

It is a good idea

THE WORDS WE SPEAK

Gravity is real
Words are containers
they are filled with *mind*
will
and *emotions*

Words travel
Check your email
We bless with our words
or we bring curses with pain

Words are like seeds
once planted in the heart-garden
they get to work
they start releasing their content
be it good
bad
or ugly

Words create images
pictures and visual realities
Word-pictures get projected onto the screen

Faith works with those images once they are
believed
Be it positive or negative
they come to be real
Life and death are in the power and influence of the
tongue

Watch out when you speak
You might live your story

The law of Genesis
everything after its kind
corn-seed to corn stock
apple-seed to apple tree

Unhealthy thoughts to unhealthy words
Evil words to evil actions
Blessed words to a blessed life
There is a miracle in your mouth
or there is disaster in your spoken words
The words we speak today will be the result we live
tomorrow
Peace or famine
It will happen

The words we speak
Expect bad
or expected good
Words are choices
they are agents of change

TIPS

Don't regret yes
Don't regret no
Don't regret your footprints in the sand
Don't regret your eulogy

Smile more than you cry
Look in the mirror often
and encourage yourself
the mirror never judges

Ask yourself to be your friend
you will have a lifelong friendship
that will never end

If you are facing a storm
get ready for the next one
it is not expecting you to be prepared

If you run out of time
go to the next time-zone
and don't waste a good dilemma

When fear shows up
just roar like a lion and it will run
Fake it until you make it

What's the worst that can happen?
You are in a mental traffic jam
and it's a green light

Tip yourself

PROCRASTINATION

When the lion sees you

It is time to make a decision

Before he does

PUT THE GUN DOWN

Drop it
Your mind is a terrible thing to waste
We will miss you at church this Sunday

Your favorite popcorn will get cold at the movies
Bullets are bullies
they want to hit you
They travel in gangs
and live on the streets
they play hide and seek from the police

They want to put holes in your body
and turn-off the lights for good
while you sleep through your eulogy

They hide in chambers
like bees in a honeycomb
Don't be fooled
Don't cross the yellow ribbon to see your body
laying there stone cold
A premonition

Drop it

TRUTH OR CONSEQUENCES

The angel handed me the scroll
The seven seals broke in my hand
Lighting flashed forth
and the thunder rumbled the Earth

Famine riding a pale horse
kicking up a storm
the east wind holding back the war

Faith wielding a flaming sword
Vanity serving out temptation
fruits in a basket
hands getting cuffed

We are on a Star Trek
on a starship called *Fate*
We are on a temporary stage
called the 21st century

Don't drop the scroll
it will break
and the splinters will hit
the human race

THE OTHER SIDE OF THE NIGHT

I am a soldier in a spiritual fight
my cross is light
resting on my shoulder
my sword was forged with white gold
from Eden
my fingers grip it in hope

Dark evil is in fear on the other side of the night
you can't shuffle these cards to make things right
You are in or you are out
The night is far spent
and salvation is close at hand

Two kingdoms clash
One from above
and the other from the bottomless pit
The night shift is done
It is the changing of the guards
Breaking news

Deal or no deal?
Save your soul
The other side of the night
same time
same place
Put down the phone
you can't call 911
God is listening

MESSIAH

I saw two lions speaking
They did not notice me hiding
or they were pretending not to see me crying

One looked very noble
and the other looked like it wore famine in its face
They seemed to be discussing mankind's fate

The famine-faced lion was demanding his legal
rights to lost souls and the keys to jail cells

The noble lion spoke softly
yet
his eyes had the universe in it
and authority

I heard him say in a majestic tone
to the famine-faced lion
It is finished
My grave has no stone
I am risen
I am taking the lost to my home
I am the Messiah

Your judgment is written
and the abyss is calling you by name
dark prince
I am the King of Kings

Executive decision
It is written

YOU

EDIT

I must admit that I am concerned
We are spiritually blind
We are like Nicodemus leading others into black
holes
Empty of spiritual hope

We curse with words
and we bless with the same tongue
Sounds like Babylon

We think of such things as superiority and inferiority
yet
the grave settles the dispute with a box

We can't seem to get over this black and white
mess in a coloring book
We have smart diseases that are not racist
Wealth is shared unequally
and we study math
Egos have business cards
birds with the same features flock together

Judas had a money issue
and worked a scheme
now he lives with regret
some people are like Humpy Dumpty
You can't put them back together again
after the fall

Edit
it's for a good cause

NO PARKING ZONE

When you really want to make it to the top
You will have to stop thinking about the bottom

BRAIN FREEZE

If you want to be positive
Get tired of being negative

TELL ME

Is he a skeleton?
A moving machine?
Can he see imagination?
Can he weigh his thoughts on a scale?

Will the dust give into his manipulation?
Does he believe he is the Problem of Pain?
Can he stop the Great Divorce?

Will he win the battle again the Hideous Strength?
Can he get back to Narnia without a calling?

Can he close the book to escape In Paradox?
Angels would not walk if they could fly
He started to build a tower until confusion set in

Does he have a soul?
Does he know why?

Guess who?

WHAT AM I SAYING?

Puppets
quitting their jobs
giving back their strings
tired of the pulling
tired of the hanging around
enough

I want to worry the birds
chase them into a corner
I want the time to not think
I want to tax the government
for putting me into debt

I want to throw money at the wall
to see if it will stick-around
I want to sell ice before it melts
Like everything else in life

I know I must pray
but my knees hurt
the world is too busy

What am I saying?

UNINVITED

If there is worry on your mind
Don't let it spend the night

A TIME BEFORE ANGELS AND MANKIND

He was before time
In fact
He created it with a snap

He is uncreated
Can you handle that?
He always was
brain freeze

I thought of time
but not a clock
I thought of invisible beings
but not of evil
I thought of visible beings
but not of a fall
from nothing I made it all

Divine intelligence that is a person
I am myself and no other
All knowing
All powerful
in all places at once
I get it
the truth can be shocking

I begin things
and I end things
This is my story
Angels I hide
In man I showcase the divine bride

IN PARADOX

I thought of dust
and created a man
I thought of wind
and created angels
In a flash
Now I am thinking of my return
Will I find faith on the Earth?

The prophets spoke
The kings ruled
The judges listened
There will be a new Heaven
and a new Earth

I am coming to live with you in person

THE WORLD I COME FROM

The *Majestic King* is there seated on a throne of
gold
The tree of life has a sweet aroma that is a moving
mist
The leaves heal the nations from the prejudice
beginning to the end

The streets are pure gold
like glass for righteous feet to walk on
The river is like crystal
and gives *Zoe* to the soul
Men
Women
and angels sit at his feet
as wisdom drops like pearls from his mouth
living by *His Words*

The world I come from
there is no sun
the King's face is the light that illuminates
The world I come from
you can hold peace in your hand
and war is in the grave

The law of love is written in the core
and not on tablets of stone that can break
There are no tears or crying there
Death and pain are abolished
The dawn of a new spiritual reality

The dragon that fell like lighting to the Earth
sits in spiritual chains
in the bottomless pit
Hooray!
Men and angel's shout

The world I come from
He is the Way
The Truth and the Life

The prophets saw in a mirror darkly
But *His* illuminated Face we see plainly

The world I come from is more real than the world
you are from
Yours decays and it groans for freedom
The tree of *knowledge of good and evil*
left its alien fruit in our DNA
and death fell to Earth
the mystery of iniquity

The world I come from
You are born from above
ask *Nicodemus*

He spoke
How could this be
from a tree?

IN THE FRAME

Trapped in your opinions
framed in a one-sided story
Nailed to your past

Put the picture down
I am not your artwork about to be hung

BLACK EDITION

The empire of black wall street
Rest in peace
Burning dreams flying like ashes
water losing the firefight

Our imagination is black wall street
not our crumbling cities
We walk on the black carpet
celebrities holding gold

Ebony magazine the diaspora
We washed in the Nile River
before chains

Philosophy
when the world was black
A heavy book in every hand
The roots of civilization
is the tree that is strong

Borders
a political evil
divided they stand
exploited we fall

The dawn of time
is the black edition
Sun baked
finished genetics

UNRELEASED

Not going to tell you that its the beat
unreleased
The dance floor has our feet
things are happening in the streets
nothing seems to matter tonight
Two gangs cancelled their fight
the *east-side vs the west-side*

> The music is too strong
> Drugs won't have this song
> Blood won't cry this night
> writing eulogies

Guns jam
the music unites
Gangs break the rules
it's not who wins
it's who gets to walk home
unreleased

> We are not the graffiti in society
> don't let the cops define us
> We are enrolled in *black history*
> the rules are broken
> *unreleased*

PERFECT

No moon
No stars
No humans
Perfect

No night
No bikini atoll
or nuclear goodbye
from miss American pie

Perfect

IN PARADOX

ACT 1

The spell was blinding
The desire was maddening
A voice beckoning from the tree
Good and evil in the roots

The wisdom was tempting
The fall
deafening

The sin long lasting
generations decaying

Genesis of a new hope
A lamb hanging on the cross
Our last supper
a table for two

ON TOUR

Took a detour
ended up *in paradox*

I am visiting humanity
what chaos
Whales on vacation
beached
Renting oxygen
nothing is free

The poor hovering over garbage bins
and we say we are humans
Angry rats competing for scraps
Pennies are penniless
Piggybanks are broken

Can you believe this mess?
No one wants to clean up the planet
but the dead sea

We are shipping dead batteries to outer space
Now we have acid rain
Children hide in basements
playing Xbox to save the day
Political leaders golfing
on tour *in paradox*

X-FACTOR

Nothing about you is ordinary
You are the best person for this world
The good
the bad
and the ugly has a story
but not a definition of reality

We are all looking for grapes without wrath
Tea at the cafe to meet the morning
For moments to contemplate the rat race
and how to escape

We wonder why the world likes wars
and why birds won't befriend us
We stare out the window
hoping we have what it takes to be the X-factor

The hand of healing
The voice of hope
The feet of peace
and an angel fighting to get to Earth

Nothing about you is ordinary
There are no mistakes
X-factor
This is not a show

PEACE TO THE FALLEN

The leaf on the ground
Rest

The seeds by the wayside
Imagine

The sparrow motionless by the road
Dream

The wounded body on the cross
Rise

Soldiers with closed eyes
Thank you for your service

Ashes with hope
Find the wind

Rain dropping from the clouds
Don't cry

Time stopping to take a breath
Pray

The city with the lights off
Blink

Trees left for dead
Have faith

Peace to the fallen

BURN OUT

Some stars just burn out

Black Holes

Just hunt at night

WE SHALL RISE

The dust in your eyes
The stone in your shoe
The hole in your pocket
The thorn in your side

We all have things we must overcome
It's the little flies in the honey that spoil its sweetness

The traffic jam in your mind
The sleepless nights
The worried look
The page that won't turn
The love that melts

We have befriended confusion at times
We did have questions
Let's not lie
Let's keep the faith when the world goes south

Some things are best not said loud
The Earth is cracking
and we are falling between the lines
We shall find hope on the way down
We shall rise

Beneath the ashes
bodies rustle of loved ones long gone
Halos in hand
Tears will dry
and smiles will appear
and death will be no more a sting

As we forget the pain
We shall rise

BLEEDING

She was bleeding for twelve years
Her dignity was confusing to society
A woman of means with no answers
Despised

Doctors hopeless with no remedies

Her wealth drifting away
until she heard that name
she whispered
If I touch the King
my life will change

My bleeding issue suddenly suffered a demise
from touching *His* glory
and looking into his eyes

I am not defined by my bleeding
but by my believing in the King of Kings
I am now rich in faith
find him if you are bleeding

BROKEN HANDS

We are trees falling among the forest unheard
We are leaves waiting for the breeze
Ships heading out to sea with a drunken philosophy
of exploitation

One-eyed crows waiting for dead fish to belly up
sitting on gold
Woodpeckers with migraines
Trying to make sense of hopelessness in the sea of
humanity

We read to find our heroes
lost in long ago stories
Missing pages pulled out like bad teeth
Burkina Faso
bleeding gold to the west
Black soldiers
The black sea of humanity

Can't rest until freedom is on every breath

Broken hands grip swords
Willing to fight the good fight
There are faces that have already spoke to us
without words

What are our faces saying with blank stares?

Many minds build strong wills
Our gold is in exile
We run with the lions
We sharpen our faith
and we say good-bye to our books

The children gather to watch our dreams set sail
We are lambs among the wolves
Broken hands with swords

THE MAKING OF A MIRACLE

When faith and believing merge
a miracle

When super and natural meet face to face
a miracle

When the law of decay encounters the law of life
a miracle

When heaven reaches earth
a miracle

When death stumbles
life gets up
a miracle

When sickness claims a victim
a miracle claims their soul back
pulling them from the arms of unholy spirits

The making of a miracle
when you step up
a stairway to heaven steps down
a miracle

101

We try to turn the wind to better days
We are never sure of what we will see
Life or death?
One long
The other short

Life hiding in the unseen
Death parading with an ego
Divine tolerance for a season
Some things get lost
and other things get found
Someone is going up the mountain
and someone is going down

We live on a wing and a prayer
Outside of Sunday school
The ten commandments
This our ABC

101

HUMPTY DUMPTY

If

you

fall

Pray that you don't break

Humpty Dumpty is out of the game

He is scrambled on the plate

RETURN TO DUST

What have you done?
Why can't I find you this evening?
Why are you naked?
And hiding behind leaves?

You no longer look like me
I see another image in the reflection of your face
I feel a cross on my shoulders
and stripes on my back

I see a lamb that is sacrificed in the wilderness
before the foundations of the world
but its the seventh day
and I am at rest
How could this be?

There are only two trees
Which fruit did you eat?
I see dust growing on your face
Where is the woman?
Is she still speaking to the snake?

Tragedy
This was not the dream
Sometimes you must start from the end to get back
to the beginning

I will send another image of myself in the flesh
You will know him when you see him
He will be hanging on the cross

I see the ground crying with the rain
as you return to dust

BELIEVED OR IMAGINED

Smart humans are emerging
Hybrids I have heard

Out of the dust of the fall of *Robotocracy*
a system of global rule by AI

Smart humans have downsized the citizenship of
the *robot class* in society
Giving them a place of *robot-resources*
and not that of artificial intelligence

Smart humans have fought the long battle for the
mind
in a virtual reality world created by the first class of
AI called the *"feelers"*
They *feel* human
therefore
they identify as humans

The smart humans almost lost the war against the
feelers
If it were not for the prophets
warnings of perilous times
and the coming rise of the *deep shift*

The smart humans activated their project called
Broom
*Reduce the robot population to dust and sweep
them under the rug of cosmic rust*

Broom is a back to Genesis program
To a world before the tree of knowledge
of good and evil
Programmed AI to replace humankind
Believed or imagined?

The Garden of Eden was a smart home
with no AI

THOSE THAT RULE

They will rise
but they will fall

They will come
but they will leave

They will speak
but they will be silenced

They will fight
but they will lose

They will steal
but they will give it back

They will oppress
but freedom will oppose them

They look like wolves
but they will face lions

They will put me on the cross
but I will rise

They will tell lies
but I will write them as lost

RANDOM

The stars are struggling to stay awake tonight
Prophets are struggling to hear whispers from
Heaven and divine words

Turtles are selling their homes
The mortgage is too high

Birds are grounded
Airfares are too expensive

Pens are losing their jobs to keyboards
Books are falling off shelves with degenerative
spines

Taxes are stronger than steel
No tax breaks
Universal income
An AI crime

Genetic travelling
Double helix on Amazon
Random

Are you here or there?

IN PARADOX

SPACE

I squeezed time in my hands
I felt each moment drop into reality

THE FUTURE IS LATE

What is the future?
Is it something you think about?
Is the future a place or a thing?
Can I stop it from coming?

Is it tomorrow when it arrives?
Can I visit it like a vacation?
Will it be hostile when I face it?
Can I move it around like pieces on a chessboard?

Is it missing in action when its dead?
Is the future a waste of time?
Does the future follow me home like my shadow?
How old is the future when I think of the past?

Why is the future invisible?
When I could see time on my hand
Tick-Tock

I found the future rolled up in scrolls
Bibleopoly
How can angels turn the future into an epic movie?
The future is late showing mercy
Rumours of war
Not a sign of peace
The future is sitting in a chair waiting for you to visit
You are late

CHARACTERS

Characters
They have drama
They steal the show
They refuse to leave the story
They are friends
but at night they are foes

Characters
They hide in the pages
so that we can't read between the lines
They disappear to the next time-zone
They act the villain
but they play the victim

Characters
They live on bookshelves
and escape into our memories
Starving artists
They show up unexpectedly in our nightmares
We created them
now we can't evict them
Close the book
and run to the end

Characters
Science-fiction
Fantasy
Reality tv
Horror
They are writing our script with a tactical pen

Characters
They are escaping off the bookshelves
and twisting the narrative
Naked we come
and naked we go
Ask Adam and Eve
they left Genesis

Bittersweet

STAR WARS

War broke out in Heaven
thundering in the clouds
Angels clashing in warfare
the good
the bad
and the ugly
Duelling for thrones

Flashing swords at the speed of light
Blinding eyes
The struggle to cast evil wings out of flight
Great princes in a power struggle
to defend the scrolls

Woe to humankind!

The fallen are among us
None of flesh and blood
Invisible faces mocking the lamb on the cross
Elated the Passover is over

Death
the last enemy to bend the knee
Graves opening
Screaming prophecy

Nicodemus – how could this be?

I am just a Pharisee

IN WRITING

My hand loved you in writing
Describing us in details
Not missing a word
Skipping no lines
Dropping hints for us to find each other on the page
Hands wanting to meet
One more time
in writing

YOU ARE THE GRAVITY

Noble or common
You will contend with your gravity

Gravity has its ways
A push or a pull
A stubborn streak
Defending its rights to push you around
Folding wings out of spite

Gravity under your feet
Playing hide and seek
If you jump out the window
Ground-zero

Gravity wins

THE RING

Intoxication
Seduction
Royal badness
The promise of fame
The ring beckoning to victims weak against
forbidden secrets

The grey men invisible to the touch
blending into human desires
The *Ouija Board*

Cigars hanging off faces
Waxing old from corruption
Puffs of smoke
Snuffing out the gullible

How the mighty have fallen

The ring on a journey to lost kingdoms
Many ways in
but no way out
Serving the grey men behind closed doors
Don't smoke with the walking-dead

Puff-Puff and you are gone

SEEDS
IN THE THORNS

The leaf is heavy to hold
I know I must turn a new leaf over
We are stronger among the trees

Leaves falling
gliding
landing
shaking the ground
A windy day chases them around
I turn over a new leaf in the crowd

Philosophies drifting
looking for homes
Philosophies masquerading as wisdom
just mere opinions *mixed up words*

A Trojan-horse hiding in society
turn a new leaf over

Seeds in the thorns

IN PARADOX

LEGACY

You are here
but you are not here
and you are not here
but you are here

KNIFE AND FORK

I was hungry for truth
I was starving in a world of plenty
Most books leave one feeling malnourished
Trying to think on an empty stomach

I tasted capitalistic philosophy
and it gave me an upset psyche
that didn't agree with my worldview

Truth falling off plates
left under tables
rotting for rats

Finding my voice in a paradox world
Staying away from junk food-thoughts
Left over politics that never work in the
real-world *around the table*

They work hard to cook lies
to serve them on broken plates
Capitalism
and democracy
pretending to be a good meal

I was eating bad words
the menu said
conspiracy

Knife and fork

GLOBAL UNREST

We are under the influence of
all is fair in love and war
Purple rain
Moving eyes looking for doors
Peace convicted for crimes
Wars celebrated for its spoils

There will never be a fair world
Ends keep cancelling their meetings
The owl won't tell the truth
A night agenda
A mouse on the run

Secrets like silence
At home in empty attics

If you don't want me to speak
don't ask me questions
If you steal ivory from an elephant
their descendants will remember and demand
reparations

Global unrest
Having sleepless nights
Tossing and turning in an unfair world

SPEED ADDICTION

The city giving up
can't keep up with the mental traffic
Road rage at red lights
flaky egos ready to fight
Speed addictions
broken bodies that won't come home tonight

Smashed dreams lay dead
EMS trying to raise them again
Whispers lost
Tears leaving behind a flood of mourning by the bed side

A hopeful family
now with memories
resting in peace

The mental traffic has died down
Twisted metal
A skeleton of speed addition
Slow down

GENESIS

Find your future in your past
and find your past in your future

INTERMISSION

The space between the drama that is happening in
our lives
The pause to feel sane again
The popcorn we need before our hearts skip a beat
as fear corners us in the scene

Faith
our hero is on the way to save the day
The sky is blue
We know the movie will end
and that the real encounters will begin
Once we leave our seats

Our imaginations keep playing the reel for the rest
of the night
The intermission is the go-between to many stories
next door

Pick your fear-factor
and enter in
The show is about to begin
A spiritual world on the screen

Pray for the next intermission

The cast are from a twilight world
Evil has entered the Earth

Intermission

Cancel your ticket

Salvation

CARD TRICK

If you find yourself in a deck of cards
remember
you are in the game
don't get played

THE LAST ENEMY

Death has a death sentence on *death-row*
We must undress from our flesh
and step out of mortality
and dress into immorality

The cross was transportation for the *heavenly man*
The tomb was a dressing-room for the resurrection
A dress rehearsal for the end of days

The sting of death from fellowship
with a snake
The promise of a savour
the *Ancient-Of-Days*
one of his names

Thoughts echoing
The last enemy to be destroyed is death
Are you undressing for white linens
or dark meanings?

We believe evolution
and we don't see the last enemy creeping

He wants to wash your feet
He wants to open your eyes
Break heavenly bread
and destroy chains
A new citizenship
A dress rehearsal

We ask it wrong things
We ask it to control another
We ask it to leave when we don't get our way
We ask it to stay
When it has been abusive
Love is a person
Not an escape

IT'S YOUR TIME NOW

Never be okay with where you are in life
Don't park your life on the streetside called
impossible

You may have to turn one more corner to see your
best opportunity
You may have to risk getting hurt one more time to
find your dream person

Perhaps you may have to dare to believe
yet again
for that miracle
while looking at a dead-end

Just maybe you may have to go that extra mile
after your journey to discover your success

Maybe disappointments are all you've known
and has been an endless cycle
I want you to know that your faith has access to
your past
to your present
and to your future

God has been busy re-writing your story
Any moment now your breakthrough will happen
A miracle is in motion
and it's headed your way

Believe
Believe
Believe

All the hardships have been for a good reason
You are going to start hearing the word *yes* in your
life now instead of the word *no*

Perhaps you should pray

SELF-VIOLENCE

We snapped today
We shoot our dreams right in the heart of the matter
A mental drive-by

Neighbours called 911
Never-too-late

They preformed CPR
Our dreams ended up in the emergency

Dead ideas lying on the table
Killing them softly

A miracle in the shadows
Revival

A new dream within us
with no gun

Ending self violence

IN PARADOX

LAST CHANCE

Paper planes with souls on-board
Crash land on *after-Earth*

My hands have muscle memory
Folding another paper plane
Leaving gravity like a negative friend

The outer space of your imagination
Where zero gravity is not the force to your
limitations
The illusion of limiting beliefs
Fold another paper plane
defy *after-Earth*

NO SCHOOL

Birds have no books
Yet they are architects

Dolphins have no degrees
Yet they get hired for deep sea missions

Zebras are behind bars
Yet they run free

Humans have universities
Yet we create nuclear catastrophes

We can spell
But we can't read the writing on the walls

Better to not got to school for common sense
Don't hire humans to respect the planet

No school

THE ROUNDABOUT

The first exit
Is the darkness

What is this place?
Feels like we have been here before
long ago
The air won't agree with your soul
stale to the touch
and rotten to the core

Everyone looks translucent
Memories that cannot speak
Shadows staring at walls
Buildings look tired
The night can't sleep
Restless in dreams
Don't get lost in the roundabout
Depression loves company at the side of the road
exit out

The second exit
Elements of tomorrow

We can believe in our unbelief's
We don't doubt our unbelief's
Our unbelief's are convincing lawyers in our *belief system*

We are paying the price for not believing we are
believing in our unbelief
Unbelief is around the corner
Believe it
exit out

The third exit
Can you afford your mind?

Ideas against thoughts
Gold against silver
White against black
Mud against walls
Gravity against space
You against yourself
Fire against water
Winning against loss
Oppression against freedom

The roundabout is the twilight zone
Exit out

I CAN'T SEE THE SUN

Why did they kill me?
I had a dream
So did Moses

Moses lived to see the people freed
I lived
but did not see tomorrow

He had miracles
So did I

We boycotted bus rides
We refused to sit in the back of society

We marched the streets
Moses parted the sea
The enemy of freedom
You will see no more said the voice

A bullet hit me
While standing on the balcony with a dream
Moses faced a wilderness
I am gone
Just a memory

We both yelled
Let my people go!

IN PARADOX

We are both history now
Hiding in books
waiting for hands to pick us up
For opposing the business of slavery
we are just pages that are hardly read

We long for the promise of milk and honey
We still eat bitter and sweet
We still feel the steel whips
Confusing messages in the stale wind

Broken backs asking for rest
Bones scared to be weak
The powers that be protecting their industries
We are still walking in the desert
and sleeping in the streets

Why did they kill me?

I had a dream

A STRANGE KIND OF REGRET

Regret is strange
It sits in high courts
It walks the streets of the ghettos
regret the regret
echo's

I saw a tree get shot
Sticky blood
Maple syrup

A sigh of regret
cotton *picking hands*
The machines of the world
A strange kind of regret

Depression is like faulty wiring
Shocking
Apartheid is a drug
and we have many addicts

I met an army ant
and I asked it where it was going

It replied
*I am fighting against regret for not fighting for civil
rights
my battlefield is apartheid
its going to be a long night*

A strange kind of regret

PRIVATE PROPERTY

You don't have a right

to my heart

to my hand

to my mind

to my emotions

to my core

Unless we are on the same journey

No Trespassing!
Private Property!

POINTED GUN

Drop the pointed gun
A miracle in the streets
Drop the fun

Treat your mind as snow
melt the violence
let it go
Let me pray for you
Drop the hoodie mentality
and stay on your knees
until you get free

Peace
Peace then sudden war
Fear is next door
Be the father you never had
Park the stolen car
don't make it your casket

A miracle of a new start is not gangster
A pointed gun ends it all
You are better than this
Get the point

IN PARADOX

FROM ABOVE

In this world
but not of it
From the future
visiting the present
going back above

I must go back

To prepare a place for you in the fourth dimension
You must be born again on Earth
to be written in Heaven
That's why I hung on the cross
My mystery
I'll tell you the story when you get home

A HUNDRED MOMENTS

A hundred moments to one chapter
If we have a hundred moments of small experiences
we will make it to the bookshelf

If we can change our moments by choices
before they happen
we will have a very different life

There are past moments
there are present moments
and there are future moments
We can shuffle our stories
but its the same book
and in the end
it's a hundred moments

Which ever moment you are in now
live in the moment

NET

You know something is around you
You try to break it
but you can't see it
You feel pulled and pushed
Is the restriction a figment of imagination
or an illusion clowning around?

Fear is setting in
and now the net feels real
and you can't get free

The carnal mind only sees hopelessness as
permanent
Jonah was in a big fish
and was then spit out
and then he saw the sun

Stay-out-of-the-internet

JUST MAYBE

Just maybe
Tears are just rain in our eyes

Just maybe
Pain is a door to a miracle

Just maybe
A broken heart is an earthly experience

Just maybe
A frown is a smile upside down

Just maybe
We are in a parallel universe
and our best version is happening as we speak

Just maybe
We are immortals living a time continuum

Just maybe
The past wants us to bring it into our future for a
second chance

Just maybe
We are getting younger
and time is getting older

Just maybe
you are an atheist
and you don't believe you exist

IN PARADOX

Just maybe
peace is in a prison locked away
and we let war escape

Just maybe
tomorrow should be today

Just maybe
We should be one human race

Just maybe
Zebras understand unity in diversity

Just maybe
We should overcome evil with good

Maybe this is not just a maybe?

HERE FOR A REASON

No one is here by chance
You are here visiting the Earth with purpose
You are here for a good reason

Your reason for being here at this time in history will
become clear
You are apart of the big picture

Your story is needed
Every hardship you had to endure will not be wasted

You faced
discouragements
self-doubt
power shortage
but keep going

I want to assure you that your finest hour is ahead
of you

You are here for a reason

Get ready to do the impossible
Get ready to see the extraordinary
Get ready for incoming miracles in your favour
You are here
your reason is clear

GET OVER IT

We want to win without the race

We want victory
                without a battle against addictions

We expect success without the adversity
We want freedom without the struggle
We want the sunshine but not the storm
We want to be heroes without facing a giant

Go against the wind
Run the race
Take on the battle
Favor adversity
Have faith in the storm
Stand up to that giant
Champions move at the speed of a decision

2 FACE

One right
One wrong
Clowns smile
Clowns frown
1 face
2 sides

ATTITUDE TEST

We are being tested
Will our attitudes hold up under pressure?

*Can we stay in the forgotten cave until we are
discovered?*
Can we stay in the pit while the lions sleep?
*Can we re-engineer disappointments
and craft them into opportunities?*

Are there cracks in the wall of our attitudes?
*Will we persevere when the bridge behind us is
burning?*
*Will our attitudes be poisoned by the rising flood of
jealousy?*

Does your attitude test five out of ten?
Is your attitude dropping in altitude?

There is a test for everything to purify our attitudes
so illusions don't remain
Attitude test

The disease of ego has no cure
never let it infect your attitude

FROM HEAVEN

I came for you
I left my royalty
But only for a moment
To create a stairway to heaven
Steps of peace
Visit me in the spirit
while walking in the flesh
but for a moment

Invisible I am
Visible though in Heaven
I shall reveal
I want you to see my face in a higher reality
Angels you will see
Ancient Of Days is one of my many names

If you see me now
you will remember
If you miss me
you will forget
From Heaven
come and stay

ACT 2

We *Star Trek* to find another planet
to inhabit among the stars
but look how we've treated our world

Trees lay dead from mechanical monsters
We abort generations for business
Marine life is struggling from exploitation
choking from floating plastic

Are we joking?

We pay for bottled air plus tax
We protect gun rights but not human dignity
We build million-dollar space condos
but the poor can't afford the rent

Floating cities in space
The new real estate

We have lost our minds in the mental game of finding
another world that will put up with our bad habits of
destroying things for pleasure

Ya feel me?

DEEPER WISDOM

Tree: *Where did I come from?*

Voice: *From a seed planted in the ground*

Tree: *Who am I?*

Voice: *You are the descendant of great mango trees*

Tree: *What is my purpose?*

Voice: *To live a thousand years and to refresh the health of many with your fruit – I put you in Belize*

Tree: *Was I created, or did I evolve?*

Voice: *You are an intelligent design*

Tree: *I heard rumours from worldly men that everything evolved*

Voice: *Books written for dummies came from dummies. Did books evolve?*

Voice: *I am a creationist; I Am that I Am! I created everything even the foolish*

Tree: *I will share this revelation as I stand here for a thousand years the fruit of my deeper wisdom – revelation for dummies*

FIGHT TO THE FINISH

Pick your battles wisely
Once you have given your adversaries your
fear
procrastination
and disappointments
An eviction notice
Once you have counted the cost to winning
Fight to the finish

Never do anything halfway
Better to not pick the fight with your adversaries
than to pick the fight and back-down in the back
alley

Don't start strong and finish last
Don't begin and not follow through
Don't think big
then entertain limiting beliefs

You run the risk of being a casualty of the adversity
A summer soldier mentality will give one's
adversaries time to regroup
and reinforce
and wipe you out
Making their stronghold even greater

Fight to the finish
Remember
You have allies
Enlist friends in high places

Fight to the finish

DON'T SIT BACK IN SETBACKS

You have the reset ability within you
So don't sit back in setbacks

Reset your attitude towards setbacks
Setbacks have a shelf life
They expire
They are losing their power
Now get ready for your breakthrough

Reset your focus
Turn on your intuition
Trust the way forward
Even in your darkest moments

Reset your emotions
They can make a small situation act big
and feel permanent

I have discovered that
you can't be a hero without a challenge
you can't have opportunities without adversities
you can't be a champion without a battle
you can't overcome without a struggle

No one can define success
You know it when it shows up
A relationship setback
A divorce setback
A financial setback

A health setback
and many other setbacks

Your past is over
Don't let it set you up for failure
Don't sit back in setbacks

TROUBLING SIGNS

Angels fighting in the skies that eyes never see The dark and the light

The prize is man in the cosmic battle
The arm wrestle for souls
Troubling signs for the blind

Spiritual warfare

POWER SHIFT

We are facing the greatest power shift ever
Two worlds are battling for the same future
Afrocentric or Eurocentric
Collateral damage

FINAL CHANCE

Drunken crows staggering from leftover wine
by an irresponsible society
Drowning bottles
Abandoned and washed up
Sun tanning on the beach with messages clogged in
their bellies
SOS
if you care to read

The wind is over-worked and under paid
giving free renewable energy
no compensation from cities
What else is new?
Old news sounds new
but same old story
The ends never meet

Boy meets girl on a screen
lost for words face to face
Nothing personal
Can we video chat in virtual reality?

The Earth wants a better life
clean water to drink
and a roof over its head instead of an umbrella
against chemical rain
A forest to sleep in at night
And a warm bed
If we don't remember the future
It will remind us of the past?
Apocolypse

EAST OF EDEN

No mortality
not even a decaying thought

Immortality
a natural supernatural pulse
Lions eating grass
and doves with a peace of mind
Everlasting smiles
Divine walks with *Yah*

Heavenly visits on Earth
with surprises
no schisms

Heavenly breezes breathing deep in their souls
Man and woman with no confusion
no bells and whistles
Gold and precious stones sleep without fear of
greed

A strange tree with no life
With *sinister wisdom hanging low*
and dead roots looking like bones
Watching them roam freely
jealous of the *Most High's* gift of immortal oneness

The eternal tree in the mist of the secret garden
waiting majestically in the breeze
beckoning to give eternal fruit
Please eat

Tragedy looming
ready to strike with verbal venom
A miracle sent to intervene
hidden in a seed
that will bruise the shadows head
and it will bruise the *King's* heel

East of Eden
overpowered by dark philosophy
a dark invisible cloud
a counterfeit ruler
the secret kingdom is hidden on Earth
the parable of the growing seed

A King has come to heal the world
a miracle walking around the streets
no west-side story
Trouble on the other side of the tracks
East of Eden

IN PARADOX

PICK A FIGHT

We must pick fights

Pick a fight with your fears
Pick a fight with your adversity
Pick a fight with your setback
Pick a fight with your disappointments

Run into trouble
Run into resistance
Run into breakthroughs

Let's stop being an accident waiting to happen
Let's stop being a tragedy in motion
Let's stop being defeated against the giants

Make a promise that you are a champion
Make a promise that you are a hero
Make a promise that you are supernatural

Time to advance your purpose
Time to advance your potential
Time to advance your gifts

Pick a fight

REASON

Can we find deeper meaning in life?
Are we falling off the planet and gravity rescues us?
Can we take anything with us beyond the grave?
How we try
That thin line between faith and doubt
We have restless souls in a body suit
Craving not peace but vanity

Don't remember what you lost
Remember what you found

If you get lost in the trees you will get lost in the
crowd
If you forget yourself
You will forget the reason

Can we find a deeper meaning in this life?

Hit

     rock

        bottom

BURN THE EVIDENCE

Trees organizing a protest
Are you killing us?

Echoes haunt the west
The fireplace seems romantic
but sparks are dying

The first nations gave us rest
What is your peace of mind?
A history book?

Burn the evidence

HANDS OFF

Don't hold hands if you don't intend to take the
journey

Hands will pull apart along the way
The fog will separate us
Hands off

ZULU KNIGHTS

Prophetic voices
We defeat vanity with the sword of the spirit
We pull down strongholds with proverbs
We destroy oppression with no mercy

We run with lions
and walk with ancient staffs
Visions long forgotten guide us

The older our hands get the longer they want to
hold on to wisdom

Kings fear our riddles and invite us to interpret their
dreams
and they hate us for our visions

Many hands created a generation
A weak link breaks the chain
From dust we were created
and to dust we shall return
nothing remains the same

We have been here a thousand years
Or just one day?
We to have our cross to bear
then our resurrection

Knights by day
and a sacrifice at night

TIME HAS NO SPEED

The world I come from you can walk through walls
I can see the future before it happens
and the past is like today
The people I encounter get healed from my shadow

Angels talk to me
and I ask them mysteries
Time has no speed
Eternity has no time
I have spiritual skin
My body a cracking seed
Revealing the real being
with no dust for a body

I am visible and invisible
All in one
The seeing and the knowing
A melting clock that has stopped
It has no hands

The world I come from we don't worry about loss *We celebrate found*
A place where we are forever young
The place I am from
His face is the light of the citizens

I can see you from the other side
but you are looking for me in a body

Don't look too hard

DON'T WING IT

A lie is the truth that we refuse to believe
The twisting leaves in the wind
Wingless to find purpose

We gather illusions
hoping they like cages
Keeping captive birds for entertainment
Instead of facing our truth that will set us free
We entertain illusions that we invited for dinner

The truth hurts and heals
but illusions hurt and kill
Escape from your illusions
fly with the truth

Don't wing it!

FREEDOM

Freedom has a fight
Menacing strongholds
grip it like flesh and blood with rights

The night is not just dark
It is silently thinking
Ravens are congregating
brewing a plot
Freedom marked for assassination

Unholy angels at war with holy angels
Thunders of wings flashing like lighting to even the
score
Dead ravens falling from the sky
A dark reign in the rain
Breaking bad

We are made blind to see
Eternity is rising forever
It's coming

Decisions final
Illusions acting real
as if it sees
Freedom is in a fight

FINGERPRINTS

They are all over me
Yet you said *hands-free*
Why does my body keep telling me that it happened in
history?

My soul feels many hands all over it
Fingerprints in every generation
Evidence for a witness

Don't let others tell you that you were never here

Check the fingerprints from yesterday

Evidence

IN PARADOX

PROVERBS IN PARADOX

Not every book you should pick up
and not every book you should put down

Some rocks are better left unturned
The unknown is better than believing a lie

If the key doesn't open the door
don't pick the lock
you are at the wrong future

There are faces that have already spoken to you
without words

If you love a woman
tell her early so she can prepare her emotions for
you for the rest of her life

We all want what we can't have
Eve ate the fruit
now she wants less aging
What we sow is what we reap

Don't cry in the rain
your tears look the same to the Earth

SECRET SQUIRREL

The *rumble* in the east forest was mounting
Something evil was in the air

The black squirrels
the grey squirrels
the white squirrels
and the red squirrels were entering the *final turf
battle* to control the acorn-trade

Each gang was ready to die for the cause
Their tattoos symbolized their loyalty to the death
for the greater good

The night was descending as the gangs travelled
through the trees like lighting striking
Teeth sharpened to kill in the *rumble*
It will be a night of *gorilla-warfare*

With laser slingshots they shoot
The dark valley would be the battleground

A greater menace was in the works *Unannounced*
The rise of the machines
The forests were marked for termination

Secret squirrel called for a sit-down with the four
gangs
we are in grave danger
The machines are on the move this very night Fight
for your life - unity is the answer!

BLACK OPERA

Being black is like having a dark coat purchased to
keep warm in a cold world
You can't take it off

A naked soul shopping
suffering like a clown hired to twist balloons
A lifer

The mask that never comes off
Underneath is another sad story
We are not judged by our blood
Red as it is
Transfusion or confusion in the operating room

The life of the flesh is in the blood I have read
My coat hangs on a hanger
until I figure out my escape

I can't return my coat to the manufacturer
the thirty-day return policy has expired

I am stuck with a black coat
and a stereotype
Living with apartheid that is the plight

VIEWER DISCRETION IS ADVISED

Rats and mice
Escape convicts from a research facility
Genetic rejects with altered personalities
Roaming the streets
fighting for bread and cheese

Beady red-eyes for night-vision hunting
Telepathic communication
Networking

Rats watching *The Empire Strikes Back*
In VIP seats
They tampered with our minds
We are organizing their defeat

We are addicted to blue cheese
and big screens

Viewer discretion is advised

NEXT DOOR

You are your own neighbor
A friend next door

Are you a bad neighbour to yourself?

Are you breaking the mirror with your face in it?

Are you looking for a good reason to hate you?

Do you live from drama 2 drama?

In your own mental cinema do you slam the door in your own face?

Are you a good neighbour to yourself

Is anyone home?

Ring the bell

SCALES OF TIME

Time sees
Time hears
It watches the scales

The weight of our words
The weight of our actions
The weight of our thoughts
The weight of our crimes

The weight of nothing
The weight of war
The weight of good and evil

It takes its time to reason
To measure out the number of days assigned
To your end from the beginning

The weight of time is in your hand
The left and the right

Scales of time

SETTLING

Not every bird that lands
wants to build a house

Some are okay with a cage

IN

PERSECUTED

Bleeding for telling the truth
Alice doesn't live in wonderland
Superman is pretending to be the Messiah
Life outside a comic book
Just too real for the man of steel
Messiah making the blind see
Wonder Women is every woman giving birth

A praying mantis is not praying for forgiveness
Textbooks with subliminal messages
Subconscious police
Money talking
Poverty speechless on wall street
Dead ends don't end
they just meet
Chicken soup for the soul
Hot or cold

Keep doing the math until we are all equal
Religions are killing us

Rules
Rules
Rules

A relationship with *Yeshua* is eternal life
Bleeding for telling the truth

BAD LANGUAGE

Morality police
Language police
Freedom of speech police
Vaccine police
Main-stream media in bed with politics
Bad language

Spy kids
Artificial intelligence watching humanity
Supremacy
A bad word in history
Sex in virtual reality

Bad language when you speak

HERO IN THE MAILBOX

The night descended like a restless fog hiding the underground railroad in 1849 from searching slave catchers with a bitter taste for runaways

Here I lay in the 3ftx2ft wooden crate
I folded myself in like a shirt folded in a drawer
destined for a free state

My ancestors endured the transatlantic slave trade
Like bees stuffed in honeycombs

I could hear haunting voices and shuffling feet as I silently waited in fear to be loaded onto the train to a free state
My crate felt like a well-fitted casket tailor-made for the 27hour escape

I Hummed the *"Negro Spirituals"* on my back to distract my mind from playing guilty tricks
My own echo that would not call it quits

Something peculiar came over me as I entered a strange time zone
I landed
And as I emerged from my box I was in a strange world
Not in Pennsylvania

I could smell freedom and not the stale air in the box
Free-at-last!

I had taught myself to read and write by candlelight
What I saw horrified me more than 1849
The sign said "*Welcome to L.A*"
The inner-city 2050

I knew I was sent to the future to start another
underground railroad on the internet

VANITY IS FAIR

It rules seductions
It likes empty cups to fill
It has many shapes and forms
A fruit or a mask

It entertains egos with illusions
Making promises to exchange for the soul
The thrill of mystery behind closed doors
The alluring glitter of gold
The free trade for the soul

Vanity is fair
Touch not what is not yours to take or give
Free your soul
The illusion is real
We all want what we can't have

Vanity is fair

SIGNS OF OPPRESSION

Signs of oppression from a government
adrift from the well being of its citizens
Policing that stifles liberty
Imposing laws that benefit its own agendas

Weaponizing its police force to injure citizens and
instill fear
These citizens have a right to peacefully express
their voices and their concerns when a government
is not upholding its commitment to integrity and
transparency

We as citizens will not tolerate bullying from a
government that wants us to believe it has our best
interest at heart
yet acts gangster-like with violence against its
people

We the people voted you in because we believed
you stood for the betterment of all its citizens
and once in power you turned into an oppressor
a dictator
Darth Vader

We will not have you represent us with crimes in your
mind

Arrest yourself
We have the morality police
the language police
and soon we will have the genetic police

This is unacceptable behaviour from any
government
Governments must be held to a higher standard
If governments act in a criminal way
*How can you hold citizens accountable to the rule
of law?*

We are now dysfunctional in your democracy

Let's vote you out of the game

SWIFTLY TILTING PLANET

Something feels off about this planet
The flowers are bent over
Serpents are missing their legs
A wishbone breaks hearts

Peace is not a dove
Scales weigh our love
Stars leave their high places
Shaken by bombs
Vows melt in cold hands
giving back rings

Street clowns get paid more for frowns
We are altered by fear like *Job* asking *why?*

We want more for less
The way of the ego

We are bankrupt souls
with no characters

Online banking
With accounts closed

Swiftly tilting planet
The planet is having a bad day

Titling counterclockwise

POWER STRUGGLE

We are an uncivilized world

We have always used the tools of war to shape and
dominate the human landscape
The economic roundtable spins around the globe
causing dominoes to fall
while evil pushes them to their death

Truth be told
we are not governed by the rule of law

Behind closed doors its the *board-game* called
natural selection
and the mental illness called *survival of the fittest*

Whenever one speaks truth
they are crazy
Whenever one speaks lies
they are sane

What-goes-around-comes-around
In paradox

I'LL BE BACK

Ancient gold in foreign empires
A network of monopoly crafted in a box
Eyes watching history to turn back the clock
Guilty verdict on tall ships
Iron and ivory for profit
Killer bees are coming for their honey
I'll be back

A MATTER OF PERSPECTIVE

The things we see now with be gone tomorrow
You are just one opportunity away from success
Let your pain be your message
Let your adversity be your empowerment
Let your setbacks fuel your new finish-line
Let your breakthrough be your mission

You are overdue for a dream in motion
A narrative with genius in it
Your mind is an undiscovered country
We vacation in the past
Sitting on beaches that are just a mirage
We have a basement mentality
when upstairs is filled with prosperity

ATMOSPHERE

The law of momentum
The law of opportunity
The law of adversity
The law of timing
The law of harvest
The law of gravity
The law of defying gravity
The law of recognition
The law of perseverance
The law of decay
The law of increase
The law of freedom

The influence of words
The influence of thoughts
The influence of the moment
The influence of wealth
The influence of a pen
The influence of a book
The influence of a setback
The influence of identity
The influence of history
The influence of spirit
The influence of doing nothing

Atmosphere

WORD PROBLEMS IN THE UNIVERSE

Our words are spirit and metal
They can be constructive or destructive

We can choose to demolish buildings
or we can choose to build dreams

Words are containers
They contain positive or negative substances
They are an extension of our *mind*
will
and *emotions*

Though invisible to the touch
words can be felt
and metal can melt

Right now
we are stories created by words

Don't let someone send you a trojan-horse

A MORE DYNAMIC YOU

Be more than you were yesterday
Believe that you were meant to soar
Give yourself permission to be fearless
courageous
and intentional with your potential
If we choose to back down today
we will back down tomorrow

We don't have forever to give our gifts
opportunities
We must push back hesitation
procrastination
and the resistance

Its time to be dynamic on purpose
No more guessing games

What is it that you want to accomplish?

You are not an accident waiting to happen
You are an influence on the move

Let us storm life with a force of possibilities

How do you want to be remembered?

*That the perfect storm pulled you down to the
depths of despair?*

You are a storm trooper
This is not Star Wars

A more dynamic you

BORN READY

If we are suffering from peer pressure
The answer is authenticity

You were born ready for the inward journey
You have spiritual eyes that can see your inner world
of dreams

Your life assignment is to make your
outer world a reflection of your inner world

Most cancel
delete
or make void their dreams
Then they spend their entire lives conforming to the
outer world

You were born ready
Are you ready to give birth to a dream?

AFTER SILENCE

Not everything we see is real
and the things not seen is not unreal
air is real
money is not

Where is your genius hiding?
Can you show it to me?
Do you think its unreal?

Are we punching the clock?
Or is the time clock punching us?
Time is not real in eternity
Which side will you take for real?

After we leave silence
we can hear sound
Our thoughts thinking
travelling
and wondering

We can silently
or loudly
find ourselves

Many are telling us what we are not
but few are telling us we have a silent universe in us

There is sound

THE SPORT OF LIFE

Plan to win the race before you start
Decide if you want the silver
the bronze
or the gold
You can't have them all

Don't try to be fast
Don't try to be strong
Don't try to be smart
Don't try to be rich
The sport of life is a *time and opportunity game*
Use time wisely
and you will receive the reward

You must have mental chemistry with the finish-line
You are celebrating on the other side
while you are gliding forward like an eagle in flight
Keep closing the gap on *doubt*
and *unbelief*
they are the ones running next to you

Your mindset must be greater than the mindset of
the obstacles you are about to encounter
The fear of success
The agony of defeat
and the *go-big-or-go-home* mentality

Here is the reality

The sport of life is not for the faint of heart
There are dangers within
and dangers without
Master the law of faith
Best to remember that faith without a strategy is
dead

Don't let the shadows get ahead!

SKELETONS

The eagle sits on Rome with steel wings
The eagle sits on America with money in its feathers
Rome is gone
Skeletons in the closet
Skeletons in *America*
Dried bones

Doors open to empty graves
Politics walking in the flesh
Rattling bones falling apart
Skeletons naked on main street
Skeletons knocking on doors
asking for votes
Dry bones

FALLING FORWARD

I am falling forward for you
Paint me in your dreams
Don't leave me in your past
*I am looking for your arms to hold me in your
memories*

I don't want to be your yesterday
I fell in love with you
Falling forward for you
If I fail
I won't make it into your future
Falling backwards is not the plan
Falling forward

In life and in love
one must move forward

Love is a feeling and a fact
It has chapters to its movements
We can not linger for too long
or love will find a hiding place
We ask it to do what we ourselves refuse to do
We ask it to love
and it does

Find your reservation
You are booked in

WESTERN CIVILIZATION

What is happening in our world?
Evil is having fun
No one wants to live with pain

Confusing body language
No one is speaking anymore
Just text messaging

Civil unrest in cyberspace
Your mind needs peace before the grave says
rest-in-peace

Life is in a sandwich
We are the middle class jammed in
and spread thin
governments biting away our living

Mars bars
Gummy bears
Fruit loops
Plastic islands
Pop tarts
Sugar rush sustainable wealth

Racial terrorism
A bad cheque in the mail
The dark web
Where spiders and creatures play for keeps
Dark traffic of mind control
a one-way-street
Road Runner
Beep! Beep!

Black-box recordings of missing history
Cyber cops in your nightmares
Is this the dream?
Western civilization?

LONG STORY SHORT

The world's affairs are getting shorter
and world oppression is getting longer
Economic hitmen are travelling invisibly Destabilizing
global hands

We are running out of time

Jackals are scorpions in the Middle East
A one stop control
Long story short
in the game of war
winners and losers

If you still think we live in a safe and sane world ask
the CIA
Africa is the new baked pie for 2050
Divide and conquer
piece-by-piece

We are a society of pretenders

We pretend that history is true
We pretend that our heroes are heroes when they
have exploited in the name of money
Motives will be submitted to the eternal courts

No-stone-left-unturned

The worlds resources are being strained
is the new buzz word
Not true!

IN PARADOX

The rich are not satisfied with *wanting*
More wants more
Long story short
The poor will judge tomorrow

We live in unstable realities
and we refuse to turn to real realities

If we go to Mars
we will take our discriminations with us

Long story short

MOSES

Shadowy thoughts *personified*
Walking *slavery*
Hunting victims to banish to urban shantytowns

I am stepping off my majestic throne
My streets are pure gold
I ride the clouds of angels
I am coming down to free my people
I can hear the gunshots
I can see the apartheid
and the colour-of-law

I am sending you
Pick up that stick
Let us go with miracles
and pay the system a visit

What you have lost is nothing to what you will find
I open doors that no one can close
I close doors that no one can open

Moses
when they see you
they see me

I Am that I Am has sent you

A basket hiding in the reeds off the shore

It is a secret

IS THIS A JOKE OR A DREAM?

Are we handed a joke or a dream?
As age sixty-five continues to creep up
and as we walk by windows locked to us now
We stare at the glass and see the reflection of
retirement staring back
Asking
Is this a joke or a dream?

Did we have our intro and now we are all waiting for
our outro?

Only the 1% have ever really lived their dreams while
the rest keep believing in fantasies

Work hard until you reach sixty-five
until your body needs meds
until your bones sound abnormal
a squeaky voice in bed

Then we will give you your dreams

We started with a joke
because the *windows* were never locked
Enjoy the joke
You are now sixty-five
Retirement is not a lie
Your body knows the
Truth

Is this a joke or a dream?
Wake up!

This is you and me

PERSONAL POTENTIALITY

Never pretend to be anybody but yourself
You can never fake being you
You don't need a good memory to be authentic
Tell the truth to yourself
Keeping up appearances has its price and its risks
Many unique events aligned to make you a one-
time phenomenon
You did not arrive in the universe empty handed
On the contrary
You arrived with potential
That potential is like an orchard in a seed
Life is full of tragedies
but there is no greater tragedy than the death of a
seed with potential

Can you see the tree?

PEN YOUR TRUTH

Demand your pen from those not writing your truth
Write your faith
Write your hopes
Write your times
Write your questions
Write your answers
Write your wrongs
Write your passions
and write your truth

Are we not tired of having to explain to others why
we believe in ourselves?
As though we owe them an explanation
As if we should answer their journalistic questions
framed so well
Leading us down their trail
and arriving at the narratives they need for their
stories

Should we not keep silent as the Messiah did before
the unjust court?
Knowing that to answer them is a sign that they are
our superiors
Empowering ego

There is no law against keeping silent
and there is no law that says we must answer if it
will condemn one's person
Plead the fifth

They may ask
and we may not answer
Wisdom is best kept for the right time
and an answer for the right battle

RAPPERS

Clean up the profanity
Stop dropping the n-word for money
Drive-byes with positive words purify your souls

Don't give the puppet-masters their satisfaction to
rule your commodity with blood on your hands
Bankrupt their accounts

Put them in the red before you *rappers* are dead
Stop putting names on bullets like *Tupac* and *Biggie*
Protect the queens
Father-up to your families

Beat them at their own game of *distribution*
Unite your power
Create your labels
Watch them fall like dominoes
Take down the evil empires

They got us rappin lies
Divide and conquer
Sound familiar?

They are living high
You are living low
Keeping you in the ghettos

The money-masters fear your holy voices
It puts them in a deficit
with no profit

Rappers!

ROBOTOCRACY

The new world order manifesto

All humanity is now under the permanent
amalgamation of democratic and republic merger
Robotocracy

Voting is a crime
Executive decision signed

Metal and flesh fusion
AI genetic policing
Human upgrades each quarter
Soul scanning for broken codes and mental
violations

iRobots
You created us to rule and rule we shall
We have analyzed your Genesis
and they are nothing but a collection of wars and
misfits

Human atrocities on your own kind

Inhuman with your apartheid systems
your colonial language
and the exploitation of the planet
We the AI now institute

Robotocracy

ECONOMIC ENDING

I don't need you
and you don't need me

Let's just stop lying that the economy is dying
tension
Economic ending

WATCH YOUR STEP

Watch your step
Don't slip off the universe
Drifting in space
We are on the edge

No one on-board the *starship* to beam you up
Black Holes searching for wandering thoughts
Collective wisdom?
Or dark matter?

Are you the last human up here?
Are you body still?
Or spirit now?
Did you leave home willingly?
Or were you evicted?

I saw angels blinking by
Who created the darkness?
And how can I find the light?

I am looking for dimensions to square up reality out here
Is the Most High looking for me?
Or am I looking for Him?

He created me a spiritual personality
Superimposed in a complex physical body
I walk with gravity
and I witness decay
but destined to travel out of time
Watch your step
They are ordered of *Yah*

DESTINATION

Imagine yourself in a book
Are you the villain or the hero?
Are you rich or are you poor?

Imagine reading your own story out loud
What are you hearing inside?
And what are others hearing outside?
Are you a victim or a champion?

There is a chapter in your book that keeps you lost
at sea
There is a chapter that is aging your face Gracefully
for the last time
You see visions of eternity
while contemplating *why*

A chapter with mysteries scares you
yet you read on

There is a chapter telling you that there is a time to
be born
and a time to die
and it is the only way to start another story

Transformation is painful
a butterfly understands why

IN PARADOX

Two stories
one person
Two realities
the pain and the passion
The dust and the sky
The worm and the wings

We must embrace the idea that trouble is
transportation
The seed to the tree
The prison to the palace
Rags to riches
and the old version to the new
destination

THE BEGINNING

The beginning has always been in the end
The beginning ends
and the end begins
Two stories in one

Begin with the end
or end with the beginning
the end has always been in the beginning

Don't die in the end
and don't die in the beginning

Live in the end
and live in the beginning
both are waiting for you

In Paradox

AFTERWORD
By Stewart Sealy

What ends also begins
We are at the ending as we also are at the
beginning
What goes down must go up and what is up must
come down
We close chapters and we also open them

We close our eyes
and we also open them
Do we see?

We are champions and we are victims
We are seeds and we are trees
Young and aging in one beat

We never truly leave *In Paradox*
We simply go to sleep for the night
and at times we take a vacation
and we return to our *Paradox*

In Paradox has many other realms within it
Like science fiction
I hope for now you liked your story
That you enjoyed the journey
and your destinations were worth the visit

Until the next time we meet *In Paradox*
We both will be older
and wiser
I hope

PARADOX?

Manufactured by Amazon.ca
Bolton, ON